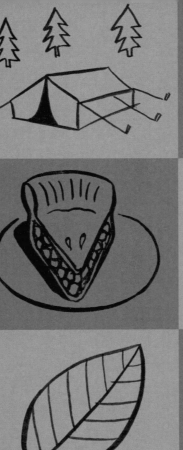

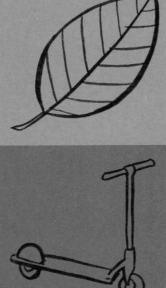

YOU!

What Makes You HAPPY?

by Amy Young

Helen DeVos Children's Hospital was established in 1993 to fill a
critical gap in West Michigan healthcare – the need for a hospital devoted to
infants, children and adolescents. More than 15 years later, it has become a
recognized leader dedicated to improving the health and lives of children
and families. One of the driving forces in making this hospital a reality
was the commitment of Helen DeVos. The children's hospital family would
like to honor Helen for the vision, kindness and generosity that will
continue to impact our community's children for generations.
This book was created to thank her.

To Paul, who makes me happy. A.Y.

This book is printed on 100# Endurance Silk text, which was partially donated by UPM.

Amy Young is the award-winning author and illustrator of many books for children. Learn more at www.ayoungart.com

For further information about Helen DeVos Children's Hospital, please visit www.helendevoschildrens.org

What makes you happy?

Is it strawberry ice cream
with chocolate sprinkles,

or climbing tall trees?

Do you love to daydream,

or listen to the world
when you are underwater?

Conner, Jason and Ahmad
are happy when they are playing soccer.
They yell "GOAL!" when they score.

Sam is happy when he paints with bright colors.

Abby hugs her puppy, Noodles.
She loves to feel his scratchy
whiskers against her cheek.

Keneesha loves to dance.
She is happy when she is

spinning,

twirling,

leaping,

whirling!

What about you?
Do you **run, run, run** like the wind?

Do you love the boom and dazzle of fireworks in the night sky?

Do you plant a
seed and watch it

grow,

and grow,

and grow?

Lydia loves to play dress-up
with her best friend Yolanda.

David and Zeke play castle-town. Sometimes
they save the town from a fire-breathing dragon.
Other times a friendly dragon saves the town.

Emily has lovely tea parties.
She invites *everyone*.

Ben loves to help his dad.
He is great at spraying the hose.

Do butterflies in the garden
make you happy?

How about frogs that say
"ribbit, ribbit"?

Do you love cupcakes with extra frosting?

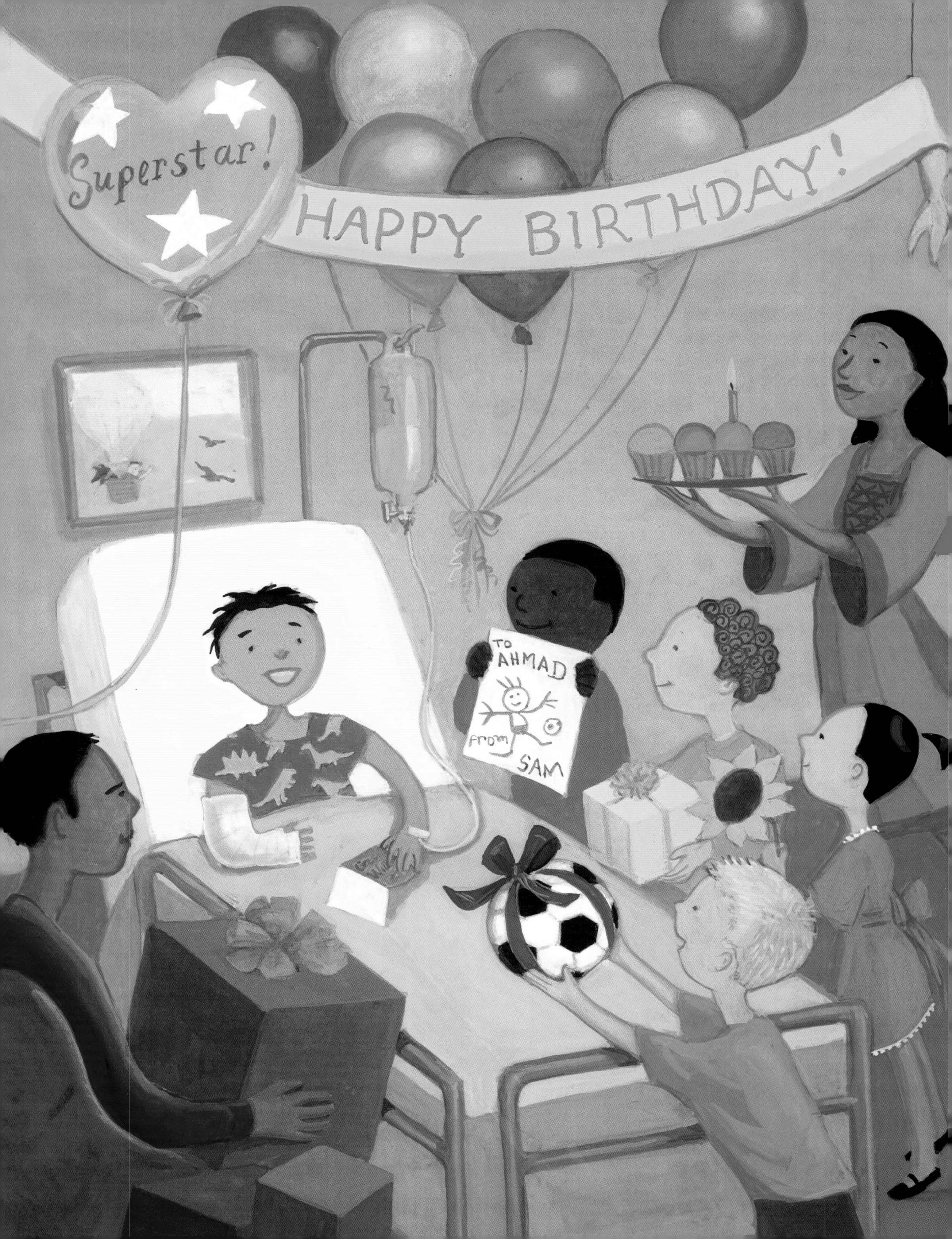

Superstar!
HAPPY BIRTHDAY!
TO
AHMAD
From
SAM

Sometimes a party is
just what you need!

And sometimes the best way to feel happy
is to make someone else happy...

...all it takes is a kiss.

What makes *you* happy?